A Giant First-Start® Reader

This easy reader contains only 41 different words,
repeated often to help the young reader develop
word recognition and interest in reading.

Basic word list for *Five Little Kittens*

a	good	play
and	here	rest
are	I	says
awake	in	screech
basket	is	sleeping
bird	kitten	squeak
can	kittens	the
cannot	little	there
climb	mouse	to
dog	now	up
down	of	want
five	one	wants
four	place	woof
full		you

Five Little Kittens

Written by Sharon Peters

Illustrated by Amye Rosenberg

Troll Associates

Library of Congress Cataloging in Publication Data

Peters, Sharon.
  Five little kittens.

  Summary: An energetic kitten can't find a good place
to play.
  [1. Cats—Fiction] I. Rosenberg, Amye. II. Title.
PZ7.P44183Fi   [E]   81-2317
ISBN 0-89375-503-6   AACR2
ISBN 0-89375-504-4 (pbk.)

Here is a basket full of kittens.

Five little kittens in a basket.

Four are sleeping.

Four want to rest.

And one is awake.

Now there are four.

And one wants to play.

"Here is a good place to play," says the kitten.

"I can climb up here."

"I can climb down there."

"Squeak! Squeak!" says the mouse.

"You cannot play here!"

"Here is a good place to play," says
the kitten.

"I can climb down here."

"I can climb up there."

"Screech! Screech!" says the bird.

"You cannot play here!"

"Here is a good place to play," says
the kitten.

"I can climb up here."

"I can climb down there."

"Woof! Woof!" says the dog.

"You cannot play here!"

Five little kittens in a basket.

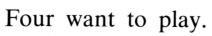

Four want to play.

And one wants to rest!